E
RAY

Rayner, Mary

Mr. and Mrs. Pig's
evening out

$14.95

97-0206

DATE			

MR AND MRS PIG'S EVENING OUT

Mary Rayner

ATHENEUM NEW YORK

For Benjamin and William

Atheneum
Macmillan Publishing Company
866 Third Avenue, New York, NY 10022
Printed in Hong Kong
5 7 9 11 13 15 17 19 20 18 16 14 12 10 8 6 4
LIBRARY OF CONGRESS CATALOGING IN PUBLICATION DATA
Rayner, Mary.
Mr. and Mrs. Pig's evening out.
SUMMARY: Mr. and Mrs. Pig's new babysitter is
not what she seems, but their ten piglets prove
masters of the situation.
[1. Pigs—Fiction] I. Title.
PZ7.R2315Mk [E] 76-4476
ISBN 0-689-30530-3

Once upon a time there lived a family of pigs. There was Father Pig and Mother Pig.

And then there were ten piglets. They were called
Sorrel Pig, Bryony Pig, Hilary Pig, Sarah Pig, Cindy
Pig, Toby Pig, Alun Pig, William Pig, Garth Pig and
Benjamin Pig.

One evening Mother Pig called the children to her as they were playing all over the house. "Now piglets," she said, "your father and I are going out this evening."

There was a chorus of groans.

"Not far," said Mrs Pig, "and I've asked a very nice lady to come and look after you."

"What is her name?" asked William Pig.

"I don't like babysitters," said Benjamin.
"Oh," said Mrs Pig, looking vague, "well, she's coming from the agency so I'm not sure what her name is, but you're sure to like her."

"We didn't like the last one from the agency," grumbled Garth.

"I'm sure you'll find that this babysitter will be very nice. Now get along into your baths and I'll come and tuck you up before we go out."

The piglets took as long as they could having their baths and made a great many puddles and splashes in the bathroom, but at last Mother Pig got them upstairs.

Just as she was putting on her best dress, the front doorbell rang. Down ran Mrs Pig, grunting and puffing in her haste, to open the door.

A dark face peered at her, heavily wrapped in a macintosh and hat.

"Are you Mrs Pig?" asked a gruff voice.

"Yes," said Mother Pig brightly. "Do come in. The children are just getting into their beds. They sleep in bunk beds," she explained, and so they did. Two to a bed, head to tail, stacked five beds high.

"Can you help me?" called Father Pig from the
bedroom.

Mrs Pig hurried upstairs. He was just putting on his
smart shirt which he always wore when they went out.
It was dark blue, and Mrs Pig liked him to wear it
because she thought it made him look thinner.
Unfortunately the buttons *would* keep coming undone,
so that everyone always noticed how very tight the
shirt had become. Mrs Pig struggled to get it done up.

Suddenly she remembered that she had not asked the babysitter's name. She ran out of the bedroom again.

The babysitter was just settling herself comfortably on the sofa.

"Would you mind telling me what you are called?"
said Mrs Pig. "The children do like to know."

"It's Mrs Wolf," said the babysitter, crossing a pair
of dark hairy legs and getting out her knitting.

"Oh thanks," said Mrs Pig, without thinking. "Now
Mrs Wolf, I've left the kitchen light on and if you
should feel like making yourself a hot drink or having
something to eat later in the evening do please help
yourself."

"Thank you, I shall," said Mrs Wolf.

At that moment Mr Pig called through to say that he was quite ready, and with many farewell kisses and hugs for the children Mr and Mrs Pig went out for the evening with light hearts.

Mrs Wolf sat in the living room and read magazines and knitted. The piglets all seemed to have gone off to sleep – she went upstairs once to check. It seemed a very long evening. There was nothing to watch on television.

After a while Mrs Wolf began to feel empty, so she went into the kitchen. But she didn't turn on the kettle. No. She turned on the *oven*. Then she tiptoed up to the piglets' bedroom.

In the lowest bunk bed were Garth and Benjamin,
snoring faintly. Mrs Wolf looked longingly at Garth,
all rosy, plump and pink.

Then she snatched him up and carried him off
downstairs. He made such a snorting and a squealing
that all his brothers and sisters sat bolt upright in bed.
Whatever was going on?

Quick as a flash Sorrel cried, "After him everyone, Mrs Wolf is not to be trusted."

Seizing Garth's blanket off his bed, the nine piglets galloped downstairs as fast as their short legs would carry them.

They were in the nick of time. Mrs Wolf was bending over the oven with her back to them, holding Garth, about to put him in.

"Four of you take this side of the blanket, four that,"
hissed Sorrel outside the kitchen. The piglets did as
they were told.

"Now!" ordered Sorrel. They ran in and threw the blanket over Mrs Wolf's head. She backed away from the oven still holding Garth. Muffled snarls came through the blanket. The piglets held on tight. Mrs Wolf struggled and threshed but she could not get out. She dropped Garth and went down on all fours. Garth wriggled free. The piglets hung on.

Mrs Wolf braced herself and humped her back, her
long hairy tail lashing from side to side. Terrible growls
came from her.

"Hang on, everyone!" shouted Sorrel. Mrs Wolf
leapt into the air. The piglets were tossed to and fro
but still they hung on bravely.

As soon as they were back on their feet they circled round her so that the blanket was wrapped tighter and tighter.

Then they tied the four corners together so that she could not possibly get out, and left her in the middle of the kitchen.

When their father and
mother came home the
ten piglets told them
what a narrow escape
they had had.

Father Pig went out
into the night and
carried the blanket
bundle to the middle of
the bridge. There he
leant over the parapet
and shook Mrs Wolf
into the swirling depths
of the big river.

And she was not heard of again for a very long time.